I0749192

MITTLE-MITTLE

TAHIR SHAH

MIGUEL ÁNGEL
VÁZQUEZ VILLAGRASA

MITTLE-MITTLE

A Teaching Story

TAHIR SHAH

MIGUEL ÁNGEL
VÁZQUEZ VILLAGRASA

MMXXIV

S
M

Secretum Mundi Publishing Ltd
124 City Road
London
EC1V 2NX
United Kingdom

www.secretum-mundi.com
info@secretum-mundi.com

First published by Secretum Mundi Publishing Ltd, 2024
A version of this story originally appeared in *Scorpion Soup* by Tahir Shah, 2013

MITTLE-MITTLE

Artwork drawn by Miguel Ángel Vázquez Villagrasa

A CIP catalogue record for this title is available from the British Library.

ISBN 978-1-915876-03-4

VERSION 12012024

Visit the author's website:
Tahirshah.com

Halwa may nurture the body, but stories nurture the mind.

Arab saying

Teaching Stories

When I was small, I was told stories from morning till night.

I was told stories about genies and witches and about great birds that could carry away elephants on their wings… and stories about distant kingdoms and magical lands ruled by warrior kings.

I was told stories of good and bad… stories of hope and others of despair.

I was even told stories about stories.

And all the while, I listened, amazed.

The more I listened, the more my mind worked… and the more I came to understand that these stories had a power about them, a secret lifeblood all of their own.

They were magical instruments, machineries that could alter states of mind and change the way we think.

But most importantly of all, stories can teach us, without us realizing that they are doing so at all.

Part of the default programming of man, stories are within us all.

Born into us, they make us who we are – they make us human.

Since earliest childhood, I have feasted on stories as a way of learning about the world, and learning about myself. They have been my dictionary and my encyclopaedia, my classroom, my guide, and my very best friend.

To descend down through the layers of stories is to be reborn, into a dominion of fantasy – one touched by real magic.

Pre-eminent within the great treasuries of tales, it is teaching stories like this one that have shown me the path to follow beyond the next horizon, and have made me the man I am.

Tahir Shah

There was once a kingdom in the Horn of Africa where all the men were brave and all the women were beautiful.

Encircled by desert, it was a land
of great abundance and verdure.

The grass was the colour of crushed emeralds,
the flowers dazzling pinks, reds, and blues,
and the air crystal clear.

At one end of the land there was a mountain capped all year round with blinding-white snow and, at the other, a forest impenetrable and dark – the Forest of Empty Souls.

There was no king, because over centuries the people had found that they did better without a leader.

The last king had passed away without issue, and it was then that the citizens decided they didn't have any need of a monarch at all.

When there was a difficult matter to be dealt with or decided, they went to a pool in the palace – a pool filled with toads.

And with great reverence,
they consulted the toads.

Although no one in the kingdom could speak the language of the toads, they found the creatures seemed to understand what they were being asked.

Through croaks and twitches of their wart-covered bodies, the amphibians managed to make their feelings known.

Now, in the kingdom there existed a special shrine. There was no religion as such, yet the shrine was worshipped night and day, and revered like nothing else.

A thousand and one steps crafted from porphyry led up to the central chamber.

Each morning and night they were rinsed
with tears gathered from the populace.

As there was no sadness, or very little indeed, the people grew a special kind of onion, the mere hint of which made their eyes stream with tears.

Enormous fields of these onions were grown by the farmers for the sole purpose of rinsing the steps of the sacred shrine.

The women would take it in turns weeping
into miniature silver buckets which were borne
ceremoniously to the steps at dusk and dawn.

As for the shrine, the interior walls
were fashioned from the purest gold,
embossed with the images of toads at play.

Deep inside, beyond a golden screen of filigree, lay a simple chamber. Within the chamber was a plinth on which stood a cedarwood box the colour of walnuts, all cracked with age.

No one in the kingdom had ever
seen the contents of the box.

It's not that they didn't want to, rather that they were so fearful that no one had ever dared to open it.

From time to time, as children drifted towards sleep, they would ask their mothers what was in the shrine.

The answer was always the same:
'There is a box, my dear.'
'But what's in it?'

Every mother in the land
always gave the same reply:
'Never you mind. Go to sleep
now and leave it at that.'

One day, a boy of eight or nine found that he couldn't stop thinking about the box.

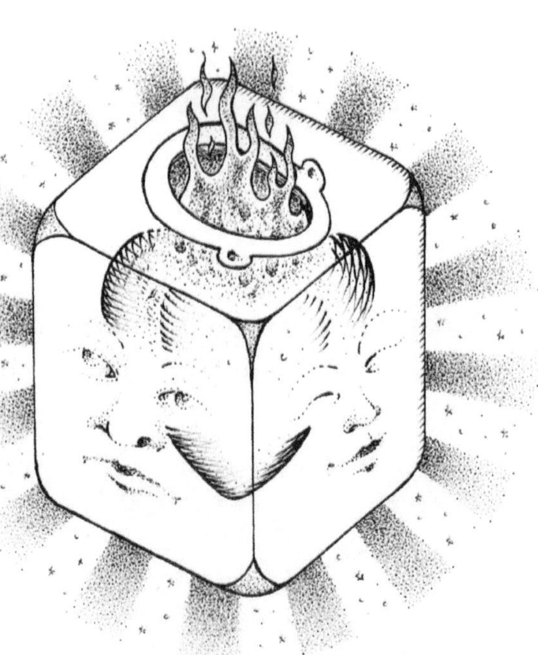

His name was Mittle-Mittle, which meant 'good-hearted' in the language of the kingdom.

He begged and begged…

… and he begged and begged…

… but his mother refused to reveal anything more than she had already revealed – that in the sacred shrine was a box, a box the colour of walnuts, all cracked with age.

Disgruntled at getting a less than satisfactory answer to his question, Mittle-Mittle decided to venture to the shrine and have a look for himself.

Next morning, when all the other little boys were huddled over their desks in school, Mittle-Mittle slipped unnoticed through the streets.

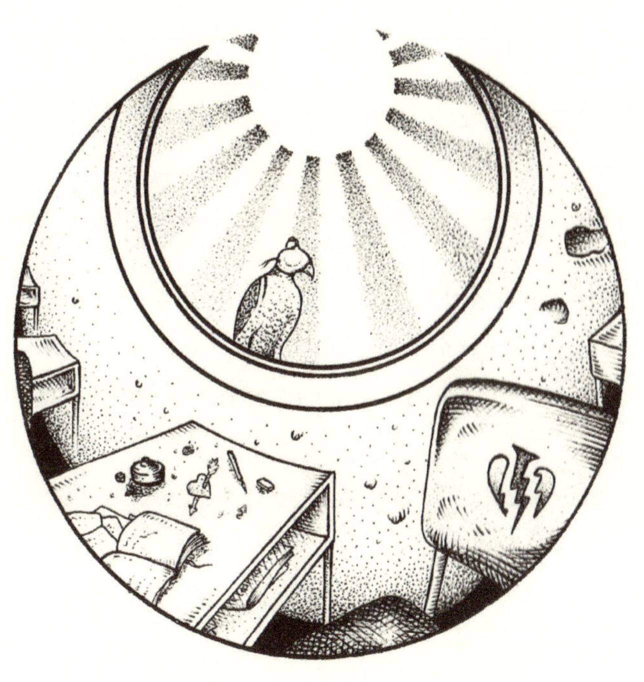

He passed the Toad Palace and scampered up the great long staircase, just as it was deluged in a rinsing of fresh tears.

The guards didn't notice the boy
because they wore special helmets
which made seeing anything shorter
than themselves very difficult indeed.

With care and on tiptoes, Mittle-Mittle zigzagged his way through the gold-walled chambers until he came to the room in which the box was kept.

At that very moment, his mother was chopping onions and blinking into a silver bucket, quite unaware that her favourite son was up to no good.

But the last thing on Mittle-Mittle's mind was his mother and the part she played in the tradition of the land.

As he entered the chamber in which the box was kept, the boy wiped a hand down over his mouth and glanced around carefully, making certain he wasn't about to be caught.

No one seemed to be watching and so,
very quietly, he crept forwards until
he was standing beside the box.

The keyhole was in line with his lips.

Reaching up, he prised the lid open,
his small fingers forcing the hinges apart.

He craned forwards,
straining on tiptoes,
holding his breath.

‘Oh,’ said Mittle-Mittle in a whisper. ‘I see.’

A few inches away in the box, laid on a bed of dusty green felt, was a nail. It was rusty, bent at one end, and appeared to be very old.

Without thinking, Mittle-Mittle
snatched the nail in his little hand.

Leaving the lid of the box wide open,
he hurried away backwards, so that if anyone
saw him they would imagine he was arriving
rather than on his way out.

In his bedroom that night, Mittle-Mittle made a careful inspection of the nail.

After a considerable amount of examining,
even with a scratched magnifying glass,
he came to the conclusion that there
was nothing unusual about it at all.

As he regarded it again, his mother slipped in to kiss him goodnight. Her face was fraught with worry, her eyes red from weeping.

‘A terrible thing has happened,’ she said.
Mittle-Mittle asked her what.

‘The sacred box in the sacred shrine
has been opened and its contents
have been stolen!

'The entire kingdom is in disarray. Every home is being searched by the guards, and every woman is weeping a little extra to rinse the sacred steps that have been so unpardonably defiled.'

'But how can the guards find what is missing if they don't know what was in the box in the first place?' Mittle-Mittle asked.

The boy's mother frowned.
'They will know,' she intoned decisively.
'Believe me, they will know.'

When his mother had tucked him in bed and was gone, the boy opened the window a crack.

He was about to toss the nail out when he had an idea. He'd often heard his father talk of a wise man who lived in the dark, impenetrable Forest of Empty Souls – a wise man who wore an amulet made from a dodo's skull.

The wise man would know why there was such an ordinary and unremarkable nail kept in the box.

Slipping on his clothes, Mittle-Mittle climbed through the window, the old nail clutched tight in his palm.

He hurried through the empty streets
until he was at the edge of town.

A little farther and he found
himself at the forest.

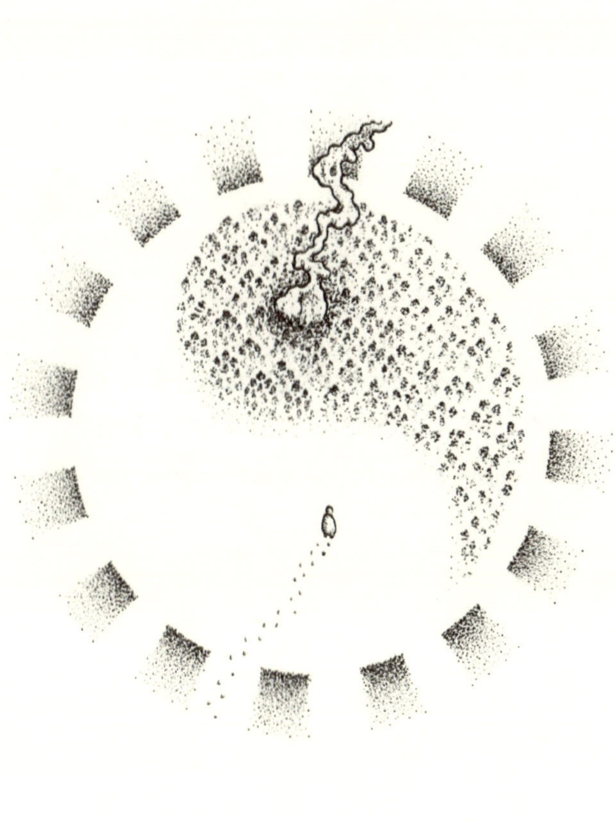

Most other boys might have felt a pang
of fear in their gut, but Mittle-Mittle
wasn't fearful of anything at all.

Slinking between the trees, he snaked his way towards the middle of the forest where he expected the wise man to live.

Meanwhile, in the town, the guards were searching from house to house, questioning one family after the next.

Eventually they arrived
at Mittle-Mittle's home.

The boy's father opened the door courteously, inviting them in.

A moment later, their son's empty bed was discovered, the window open.

Mittle-Mittle's parents were
dragged away to the cells.

Deep in the Forest of Empty Souls, an elderly man was huddled over a fire at the base of a towering green winter oak.

With eyes closed, he was murmuring incantations, scribbling figures in the air with the tip of one finger.

Around his neck was an amulet
fashioned from a dodo's skull.

Mittle-Mittle watched from a distance.

For the first time in his life, he sensed fear – not so much a fear of the wise man as a fear of something he didn't understand.

Why would the people of the land in which he lived keep an old rusty nail in a box and protect it from one generation to the next?

Very slowly, with sure footsteps over moss, the boy approached the wise man. As he drew nearer, Mittle-Mittle could feel the heat of the flames on his face.

‘Excuse me,’ he said when he was close.

The wise man froze.
He opened an eye. Then the other.

‘And who might you be?’ he asked.

‘I am Mittle-Mittle.’
‘And what do you want?’

'I want to know why the people of our kingdom keep a rusty old nail in a box, guard it day and night, and wash the steps to its shrine with tears.'

The boy held up the nail and,
as he did so, the ancient smiled,
his teeth reflecting the firelight.

'That rusty old nail is exactly what it looks like,' he said.

‘And what is that, sir?’

‘You tell me.’

Mittle-Mittle held the sliver
of iron into the light.

‘It’s a rusty old nail.’

‘Yes… and that is what it is.’

‘But is that *all* it is?’ the boy asked,
his expression sombre.

'No,' answered the wise man who wore an amulet made from a dodo's skull. 'I suspect it is far more than that.'

'What exactly do you mean?'

'I mean that, to certain people in certain places, and living at certain times, it is likely to be far more than a sliver of rusting metal.'

The boy frowned. He was about to say something, but the old man silenced him.

'Always remember this…' he said.

‘*What*? What shall I remember?’

The ancient squeezed his hands into fists and said: 'Always remember that despite imagining they are the keepers of great wisdom, the foolish tend to cling hold to nonsense most of the time.

‘A rusty nail may indeed be a symbol with a distinguished past, but it will never be more than a reflection of the ignorance of those who place value upon it.’

Finis

About the Author

Descended from a long line of storytellers, writers, and savants, Tahir Shah is one of the most prolific authors of his generation. He has published more than sixty books in numerous genres, including travel, fiction, and fantasy, as well as tales for children.

Raised in the tradition of Eastern 'teaching stories', Shah is passionate about stories and storytelling. He regards the ability to learn from folklore as being in us all, what he calls a 'default setting of humankind'. As well as having written scores of books, Shah has made documentaries for National Geographic TV and The History Channel. He is the founder and CEO of the charity, The Scheherazade Foundation.

About the Artist

Miguel Ángel Vázquez Villagrasa is a teacher, illustrator, and writer. He studied philosophy at the Complutense University of Madrid and has since written for several magazines, recently completing his first book, *El anhelo y la destrucción*. A self-taught artist since childhood, he draws inspiration from Eastern drawings and sculpture as well as European artists such as Bosch and Escher. He is also inspired by primitive and ancient art that captures the 'essential' rather than empirical experience.

Books By Tahir Shah

The Writer's Craft

The Reason to Write

Workbook: Comprehensive, Volume I & II

Workbook: Fantasy, Volume I & II

Workbook: Fiction, Volume I & II

Workbook: Historical Fiction, Volume I & II

Workbook: Teaching Stories, Volume I & II

Workbook: Travel, Volume I & II

Novels

Jinn Hunter: Book One – The Prism

Jinn Hunter: Book Two – The Jinnslayer

Jinn Hunter: Book Three – The Perplexity

Hannibal Fogg and the Supreme Secret of Man

Casablanca Blues

Eye Spy

Godman

Paris Syndrome

Timbuctoo

Midas

Zigzagzone

Nasrudin

Travels With Nasrudin

The Misadventures of the Mystifying Nasrudin

The Peregrinations of the Perplexing Nasrudin

The Voyages and Vicissitudes of Nasrudin

Nasrudin in the Land of Fools

Travel

Trail of Feathers

Travels With Myself

Beyond the Devil's Teeth

In Search of King Solomon's Mines

House of the Tiger King

In Arabian Nights

The Caliph's House

Sorcerer's Apprentice

Journey Through Namibia

Teaching Stories

The Arabian Nights Adventures

Scorpion Soup

Tales Told to a Melon

The Afghan Notebook

Daydreams of an Octopus & Other Stories

The Caravanserai Stories

Ghoul Brothers

Hourglass

Imaginist

Jinn's Treasure

Jinnlore

Mellified Man

Skeleton Island

Wellspring

When the Sun Forgot to Rise

Outrunning the Reaper

The Cap of Invisibility

On Backgammon Time

The Wondrous Seed

The Paradise Tree
Mouse House
The Hoopoe's Flight
The Old Wind
A Treasury of Tales
The Tale of Double Six
The Forgotten Game
King of the Jinns
The Destiny Ring
Changing the World
Cat, Mouse
Frogland
Mittle-Mittle
Capilongo
The Princess of Zilzilam
The Singing Serpents
The Tale of the Rusty Nail
The Unicorn's Tear
The Clockmaker Who Travelled Through Time
The Fish's Dream
The Man Whose Arms Grew Branches
The Most Foolish of Men
The Shop That Sold Truth
Qwerty
Renaissance
The Man With the Tiger's Head
The Kingdom of Blink
The Wisdom of Celestine
Dream Soup
The Skeleton Factory
An Unexpected Gift

The Problem Exchange
The Pharaoh Code
The Monkey Puzzle Club
Liquid Time
Cat Dog, Dog Cat
Princess Pickle's Laugh

Anthologies

The Anthologies: Africa
The Anthologies: Ceremony
The Anthologies: Childhood
The Anthologies: City
The Anthologies: Danger
The Anthologies: East
The Anthologies: Expedition
The Anthologies: Frontier
The Anthologies: Hinterland
The Anthologies: India
The Anthologies: Jinns
The Anthologies: Jungle
The Anthologies: Magic
The Anthologies: Morocco
The Anthologies: Nasrudin
The Anthologies: People
The Anthologies: Quest
The Anthologies: South
The Anthologies: Taboo
The Anthologies: Teaching Stories
The Clockmaker's Box
The Tahir Shah Fiction Reader
The Tahir Shah Travel Reader

Research
Cultural Research
The Middle East Bedside Book
Three Essays

Edited by
Congress With a Crocodile
A Son of a Son, Volume I
A Son of a Son, Volume II

Screenplays
Casablanca Blues: The Screenplay
Timbuctoo: The Screenplay

A REQUEST

If you enjoyed this book, please review it on your favourite online retailer or review website.

Reviews are an author's best friend.

To stay in touch with Tahir Shah, and to hear about his upcoming releases before anyone else, please sign up for his mailing list:

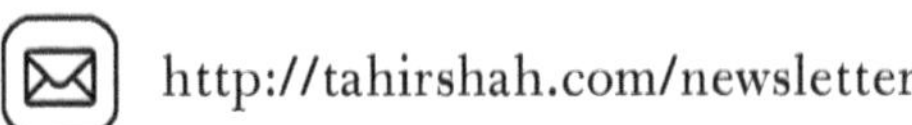

http://tahirshah.com/newsletter

And to follow him on social media, please go to any of the following links:

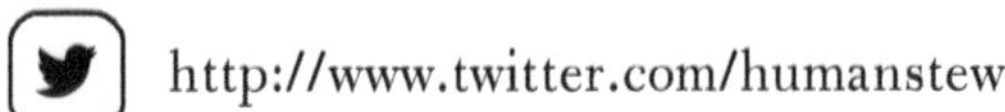

http://www.twitter.com/humanstew

@tahirshah999

http://www.facebook.com/TahirShahAuthor

http://www.youtube.com/user/tahirshah999

http://www.pinterest.com/tahirshah

https://www.goodreads.com/tahirshahauthor

http://www.tahirshah.com

www.ingramcontent.com/pod-product-compliance
Lightning Source LLC
Chambersburg PA
CBHW030522310726
48979CB00010B/1768/J